# CREATION OF A FATED THIEF

# CREATION OF A FATED THIEF

## A THAUMORIAN LEGENDS NOVELLA

A M ENO

ISBN
979-8-9893390-6-8 (paperback)
979-8-9893390-7-5 (ebook)

ALSO BY A.M. ENO

## THAUMORIAN LEGENDS

### *Novellas*

*Released*

Origins of a Guild Master

Secrets of a Sagacious Witch

Dawn of a Ruinous Love

Creation of a Fated Thief

*To Be Released*

Heart of an Outcast Mistress

### *Novels*

*To Be Released*

The Death Bringer

*To the friends that saved us.*

# CHAPTER 1

A fist connected with the side of Layshan's face, and, not for the first time during the fight, he wondered where Dai had learned to punch, as he had a dreadful form. The blow was so poorly executed it didn't even hurt.

He could have turned the fight around at any time by dodging the next blow by a hair's breadth and letting Dai's knuckles connect with the brick wall instead of his head, breaking his hand. He could have walked away while Dai wailed in pain.

Except the older boy had brought back up.

If Layshan won, they would pounce, hold his arms, and use him as a practice dummy.

One bully was easy to fight off. Even two were doable under the right circumstances. But five? Those were odds Layshan wouldn't bet on. Losing with dignity and taking the beating in stride was better for everyone involved.

Another punch landed against his jaw, and Layshan cried out, too loud to be convincing. He brought his hands to his face as though to keep his teeth in place. He made his knees shake and buckle until he collapsed to the ground, performative moans echoing through the alley.

"Next time I ask for payment, I expect you to hand it over with a smile. Got that, Air Sucker?" Fists resting on his hips, Dai loomed over the blonde-haired boy half his size.

Layshan glared, not bothering to answer such a stupid question. It had been months since he'd paid Dai his supposedly earned money. Not since he realized the older boy couldn't fight and used his size and ugly face to intimidate the other kids.

Dai continued without waiting for an

answer, enjoying hearing himself talk. "Now, I'll ask again. Where is this week's payment?"

Layshan said nothing. Did nothing. He only glared up at the older boy from his spot on the ground, his back pressed against the wall.

Dai's nostrils flared before his dirt-caked foot connected with Layshan's prominent ribs. That one actually hurt, and the world spun, Layshan's stomach lurching with it.

Falling to the side, he struggled to his hands and knees. He tried pushing himself to his feet when Dai landed on his back, sending him face-first into the filth. Dai dug a knee into Layshan's back as the other boys spurred him on, fueling his overblown ego as he put more weight onto Layshan's shoulders. The pressure cut off Layshan's airway, and no matter how much air he tried to force into his lungs, his crushed ribs wouldn't expand.

Groping hands probed his sides, searching for the patched coin purse shoved into a makeshift pocket. Dai found the pouch and pulled it from Layshan's tattered outer layer. Layshan choked on dust and dirt when the pressure on his back eased and his lungs expanded.

The pouch jangled as the boys tossed it around, each taking a share of his coins until it sagged, noticeably emptier. When it landed in Dai's hands, he inspected the remaining few coins before dumping them into his meaty palm and dropping the patched-up cloth with a flick of his fingers.

"Those are mine," Layshan mumbled half-heartedly, not bothering to sound pathetic. It didn't matter if he was convincing so long as he played his part.

"And now they're mine. Funny how that works, isn't it, Air Sucker?" Dai spat.

The howling boys started back down the alley, leaving Layshan gasping on the ground. However, once they turned the corner and he was sure they wouldn't return, he took one more deep breath before ending his pitiful performance. Brushing away the pebbles embedded in his stained pants, he rubbed his jaw and pushed stringy strands of hair out of his eyes.

His greasy mop was far too long and nothing more than a disgusting curtain hanging before his eyes, but he refused to cut it. It offered another layer of protection to hide him from his world, the lower part of the Elemental City.

Layshan picked his way between piles of trash and the other refuse at the enclosed end of the alley. With a wave of his hand, a slight breeze blew away the worst of the stench.

The alley backed up to a business built later than the alley. Due to poor city planning, the business didn't quite meet the alley wall, leaving a space between the two Layshan took advantage of.

Dai didn't find him in that alley by accident.

Counting the bricks from left to right, starting with the discolored one at eye level, he tapped the bricks one at a time until he found the one he'd loosened long ago. Pressing a palm to the brick, he pushed with his hand and magic, forcing a current through the cracks and around the brick until it slid back, revealing the top of the brick beneath. Or, at least, where the top of the brick used to be before Layshan hollowed it out to hide a second coin pouch, full and bulging.

He pocketed the pouch, squeezing it for reassurance. It only contained coppers, but he had saved every coin he could spare.

Covering the hole with his palm again, he yanked it back, taking an air current with it. The rush pushed the loose brick back into place with a grating scrape, the slight breeze ruffling his greasy hair, making the wall appear seamless again.

"You should think about investing in some friends."

The deep voice from behind him made Layshan jump. A man stood tall at the alley entrance, his shoulders pushed back with perfect posture emphasized by an expensive three-piece gray suit.

Layshan froze, every muscle tensing until even his jaw refused to move. At the edge of his mind, he tried to muster a reply, but he was too busy preparing to run at the first opportunity.

Taking slow, deliberate steps, the Kinetic

stepped farther into the alley, examining Layshan's skeletal frame.

"One of these days, they will grow tired of watching someone else have fun and take a turn themselves. And they might not stop for a few coins. Some friends, a partner perhaps, would help. Offer a bit of protection. Friends are always worth investing in."

Layshan eyed the man with each step he took, every muscle in Layshan's body coiled tight, prepared to run at the first sign of danger. He tried to meet the man's curious gaze but couldn't hold it. The old men who looked at him long rarely thought anything good, offering him a few coppers in exchange for twenty minutes of his time. They always said it like a question but never took "no" very well.

The man hadn't asked a question yet, but a shrug seemed the safest response.

"Some of those who work for me have seen you around. They told me you can fight. Why did you not just now?"

That was the first Layshan had heard of someone watching him. Normally, he stayed vigilant, keeping one eye over his shoulder to spot patterns in the people he passed. Either he'd missed something, or the people the man spoke of were far craftier than he was. Layshan searched his mind for what reason someone would have for keeping tabs on a boy whose ribs stuck out as prominently as his knobby elbows, but he couldn't think of one. The ability to swipe a coin here or there and hold his own in a back-alley fight wasn't anything special, as far as he was concerned.

Layshan shrugged again, unsure of the best reply.

The man was unfazed by Layshan's silence and, miraculously, stopped a polite distance away. But just because he was being nice for the moment didn't mean he would be nice later.

"I see. Well, if you would like, I can help."

Layshan shook his head until his jaw actually hurt.

"Are you sure? I would wager you did not work for those coins, and that can be a dangerous business to go into alone."

Layshan's fingers found the pouch in his

pocket, filled with coins gathered off sidewalks, offered by a kind stranger, or *accidentally* fallen from a pocket or two.

Layshan didn't mind stealing, but he tried to avoid it. If caught, the city guards wouldn't bother with a trial. All too often, one of the kids living in his building would go out for the day and not return. He'd stopped crying for them long ago after realizing water was too precious to waste so often.

They may not have been the most organized group of orphans, and he had to deal with older kids like Dai, who thought they were Goddess-blessed because they ate enough to grow tall and see their fourteenth year. But the building was dry, and the city guards didn't come knocking. Kids worked together, splitting hard bread and sharing tips on the best places to hit for dropped coins and loose pouch strings. The shared crumbs and information never got them far, but it got Layshan further than he would have gotten on his own. He didn't have any friends, but a few people offered him scraps in exchange for staying up all night and watching their back, and that was close enough, right?

"I'm fine," he muttered.

"My business is different—no more sleeping on the ground or hungry nights." The off-hand mention of such luxuries nearly convinced Layshan they were so accessible.

"I'd be safe…" Layshan whispered, thumbing at one of the coins poking through a fraying seam at the corner of his pouch.

The man chuckled, a light melodic sound almost self-deprecating in its understanding. "Relatively speaking. Breaking the law is always dangerous. What I am offering is a better way to do it."

Gritty teeth chewed his lip. The temptation to give in and find out if the offer was genuinely different grew with each second. If he'd learned anything, it's that when things sounded too good, they usually were. This man didn't know him and had no reason to offer Layshan such opulence. Food, work… maybe a bed. But Layshan had nothing of substance to offer in exchange. He wasn't the best brawler or the best thief. He wasn't the best at anything.

When Layshan didn't answer, the man shrugged and turned to leave, starting out of the alley and back toward the street. "The choice is yours. With me, the choice will always be yours. You may come now or find one of my people if you change your mind later."

The man turned out of the alley, his polished black shoes clicking against the stones, echoing off the brick walls.

Layshan's chance at a new life was slipping through his fingers with every step the man took. He said Layshan could find one of his people, but he did not know how. He had to make his choice, and he needed to make the right one.

Layshan ran to catch up, stepping beside the man as they walked down the sidewalk. He waited for the man to throw him a smug smirk and show his true motives or say something to shame Layshan for hesitating, but he didn't pay the boy any mind. Instead, he walked down the street with his head held high, tipping his chin to greet anyone who met his eyes. Occasionally, he adjusted his sleeves as if trying to straighten a particularly stubborn but invisible wrinkle.

Many passersby threw them skeptical glances. The two made an odd pair: a small, bone-thin, dirty boy whose shoulders hunched more and more beneath the weight of each new scrutiny, next to a man who stood tall in a well-tailored suit more appropriate for the business district.

Absently, Layshan wondered how the man wound up there, deep in the decrepit old industrial district that was as abandoned as the people who lived there. Ultimately, though, he decided it didn't matter.

# CHAPTER 2

It wasn't long before Layshan sat on a cushioned loveseat before a crackling fireplace in a low-lit, windowless library office. The man sat in a nearby chair, an ankle crossed over a knee, a thin file in his lap.

"We will work out more details later, but I am sure you are quite hungry and tired, so I prefer to make these first meetings quick. Right now, all we need to figure out is your name and job."

Fidgeting, Layshan tried not to gawk at the walls of books as his toes skimmed the rug. Sitting on the loveseat's expensive fabric had him avoiding squirming with guilt. Perhaps if he sat still enough, his disgusting clothing wouldn't stain it.

He glanced at the man out of the corner of his eye, waiting for him to flip, to become the menacing threat of Layshan's nightmares and reveal what he really wanted from a desperate boy. So far, though, the man hadn't moved to touch or hurt him. He hadn't called Layshan a bad name or said anything that might hold a double meaning.

"My name is Layshan," he croaked, unwilling to speak much louder than the crackling fire.

"Yes, it may have been. But here, you can start over, which means changing your name if you wish. Sometimes, we receive our names from people who do not know us well. Even someone who may have done us harm. You may choose anything you like."

Layshan thought back to where his name came from, to the first person who acknowlededged his existence with something more than a scowl but came up blank. Someone must have cared for him as a baby until he could care for himself, but no one came to mind—no warm smile of a mother or protective arms of a father.

He repressed the memories of where he came from, so much so that he wasn't sure they existed in the first place, forgotten in self-preservation.

He shook his head. "My name is Layshan."

The man nodded and wrote something down. "Very well. If you change your mind, you have until your first job to do so, which brings me to my next point: your job. From my under-standing, you have stolen to provide for yourself thus far. Is that correct?"

Layshan nodded, playing with his stained coin pouch, metal coins scraping together. He'd been waiting to be asked for payment, for something in exchange for the supposed kind-ness being offered. So far, though, the man hadn't asked for anything but answers and decisions.

"Do you have anything against continuing that? Sometimes, when people come to me, they want something familiar; other times, they want change."

All Layshan had ever done was beg and pickpockets. He didn't participate in some of the things kids did for money, for the chance to eat, like trafficking substances or acting as the middleman between Witch and addict, taking on the riskiest part of the trade in exchange for commission. Others handed over the only thing they owned: themselves. Rumors of a dark market circulated, said to be a place of illicit apprenticeships and a clientele who wouldn't report a missing coin here and there, but he'd never gone looking for that.

"Stealing is fine."

"Good. This can also change if you decide to do something else, and you may change this at any time. Remember, every job requires training, so you must start at the bottom if you change fields." The man spoke almost monotonously, repeating words he'd said hundreds of times. He continued to scribble in the file before snapping it shut.

"I am going to find someone to show you

around. It may take a moment; this place is bigger than it appears, so feel free to look around and make yourself comfortable until I return." Standing, he placed the file on the clutter-free wooden desk in the center of the room and headed for the large double doors leading deeper into the building.

With a wave of his hand, the doors opened and closed tight behind him.

Layshan contemplated investigating his surroundings. Pulling out books and flipping through them, or going through the file the man scribbled in. But since he couldn't read, both would be a waste of time. Instead, he stayed exactly where he'd been left, enjoying the warmth of the fire and the couch cushions while he had the chance.

Eventually, the warm, earthy scent of the crackling flames in the otherwise quiet office lulled him into a tentative comfort. Despite his wariness, he couldn't help but feel… safe. His slim, lanky limbs became deadweight, pulling him onto the cushions until he stretched across the loveseat, sinking into unconsciousness.

When Layshan woke, the fire still cackled, but a boy his age sat cross-legged in front of it, shadowed by the dancing flames. Warm light flicked off two copper coins, skipping between the boy's fingers and occasionally colliding with a metallic ting.

Layshan jolted upright, scrambling until his back pressed into the corner of the couch. Heart pounding in his chest, he locked gazes with the boy.

Where Layshan was petrified, the tip of the boy's head emphasized a playful curiosity. Feathery hair, the same color as his round, ashy-brown eyes, fell into his face. Innocence played across his face as he assessed Layshan like a new toy, devoid of any alarm at his reaction.

"Finally, you're awake," the boy chirped, jumping to his feet with a burst of energy that sent him across the coffee table between them. Perching on the edge, he thrust out a hand, letting it hang in the empty air between them, and gave a toothy grin. "I'm Ra."

Layshan stared at the hand, eyeing the eager smile, debating whether the enthusiasm was a trap or if the boy was genuinely so… happy. His lively energy was so startling that Layshan believed it had to be forced.

Slowly, Layshan reached out his hand how someone would approach a growling dog. Before he met the outstretched fingers, Ra snatched his palm and shook it vigorously. It rattled Layshan's whole body, and he yanked his hand free, fearing his arm might fall right off.

"Nice to meet ya! Your name's Layshan, right?"

Layshan nodded, still scrutinizing the fascinating new creature before him.

"Great! Let's get started. You look hungry and like you need some new clothes." Ra bounded off the table, skipping toward the office doors. He raised his knuckles to knock, then realized Layshan wasn't by his side.

An odd mixture of astonishment and apprehension kept Layshan frozen, watching the ball of energy from over the back of the couch. When faced with something new, the body chooses fight, flight, or freeze. Usually, Layshan chose one of the former two, but he was as frozen as a dripping pipe in the middle of winter.

In his experience, it wasn't normal for kids to have so much life and to be excited about… everything. The behavior was unexpected; so far from what he was used to, he didn't have a frame of reference for how to react.

Ra tilted his head side to side, studying Layshan as if he were the odd one before running back to the couch. He gripped the back and leaned in close as though he'd find an explanation written in tiny writing on Layshan's nose.

Layshan pulled back to keep at least some distance between them.

"Aren't you hungry? Dinner is downstairs; if we wait too long, snacks will be all that's left. We'll have to wait until sundown for breakfast."

Shaking his head, he tried to process what Ra was saying. It was like they spoke vaguely different languages containing some of the same words but using them in a nonsensical order.

Breakfast, dinner, snacks… those were concepts Layshan had heard of but never experienced. In his world, you ate when you had food. It didn't matter what time of day you did it.

"Are you scared? I promise everyone will be nice. No one will say anything about how you smell."

Layshan's nose crinkled. "Hey!"

Of course he smelled terrible. Ra would, too, if he didn't have a way to bathe and wore the same clothes daily for the last year.

Ra's grin widened. "I knew you could talk! You wanna see a trick?"

Layshan's mouth fell open, but no words came out. Keeping up with Ra and his rapid subject changes made his head spin.

Ra took Layshan's silence as a yes and climbed over the back of the couch, plopping down on the cushions too close for Layshan's comfort. Their knees bumped, and Ra leaned in like he was about to share a secret.

He pulled out the two copper coins he'd been playing with earlier and held them up.

They were shiny; the ridges rounded with wear and stamped with the City of Elemental's insignia.

"Ready? Watch closely." Ra waved his hands, moving them back and forth in opposite directions. Layshan watched determinedly at the risk of going cross-eyed. Suddenly, Ra clapped. The crash of smacking palms made Layshan jump back on instinct.

"It's ok. Sorry, that was loud. I didn't mean to scare you. But look!" Ra held up his hands, showing off one coin and one empty palm. Layshan forgot about his fear, intrigued by the mystery of the missing coin. He leaned in, inspecting Ra's vacant hand to look for any sign of where it went, when Ra reached out and tapped his ear.

Layshan jumped back again, his arms shielding his face against an incoming strike. But the assault never came, and when he peaked between his forearms, he found Ra holding out the second coin, grinning with pride from ear to ear. Layshan uncurled from his defensive position, probing at his ear to figure out where the coin came from.

Ra laughed, falling back against the arm of the couch. He clutched his middle with delight, his carefree joy as light as wind chimes—the contagious sound of someone who hadn't experienced a hard day.

Layshan had heard that type of laugh while stalking the shadows of the business district, watching jovial shoppers for dropped coins. Usually, he only overheard joy, picked up like a stray scent in the breeze. Yet another aspect of life that overlooked him, leaving him behind and forgotten.

Usually, the sound grated on his nerves, making him angry and jealous of how unfair life was. But from Ra, it was an invitation—an offer—a rope tied around Layshan's middle, pulling him into Ra's carefree life.

Layshan's lips twitched into the closest thing to a smile he'd experienced in a long time. In fact, he couldn't remember the last time he had a reason to smile. It warmed him more than the fire, and he wanted to join Ra in his laughter; he just wasn't sure how.

"See! It's a trick. I've been learning how to do them so I can start stealing cooler stuff."

Steal… he was also going to steal stuff, just like Layshan.

"Ya know, I like you. You don't talk much, but you seem ok." Ra proclaimed, tucking away the coppers. "Now, come on. I'm getting hungry. I swear, it'll be worth it."

Layshan's stomach growled long and loud at the thought of food. Hunger was an achingly familiar burden, but he wasn't used to food being talked of so freely. Where he lived… used to live… they rarely spoke of food. Bread and apples were the currency of dark corner deals and the topic of dreams, spoken of in hushed, reverent tones.

Ra jumped over the arm of the couch and headed for the double doors again. Layshan followed, opting for a path around the loveseat instead of over it.

The doors opened wide with a yawning groan at Ra's knock.

They revealed a grand room of such beauty it left Layshan stunned, lost in a resplendence he didn't know existed. Painted constellations mimicking the night sky stretched across the ceiling, backed by clouds and swirls of rich blues, purples, and blacks. Golden columns held swooshes of glittering fabric hung high above groups gathered around the room.

At one end of the room, cushioned chairs and a couch surrounded a fireplace, inviting him to curl into their corners. Around the rest of the room were game tables and bookshelves, packed to the brim with tomes.

"Headed to dinner?"

Layshan spun at the familiar voice and found the man from earlier sitting at one of the gaming tables with a book in his lap, occasionally looking up to study the game he was in the middle of with a teenage Anima. The boy was as clean and healthy-looking as Ra. He had pulled back his long black locs from a friendly dark face, making room for a fluffy creature on his shoulder. It studied the game board, its too-large eyes as enraptured as the Anima's it perched on.

Ra nodded. "Yup! Then to the dorms."

The man nodded approvingly, looking up long enough to move a single game piece. The move made the Anima's eyes narrow, lips twisting to the side, and the fluffy creature (his familiar, probably) squeaked, its tail flipping back and forth. "Good. Have a lovely dinner, then make sure he gets everything he needs. Extra blankets, pillows, clothes, shower things…"

Ra waved a hand dismissively. "Yeah, I know." He grabbed Layshan's hand and dragged him to a metal part of the wall with a slit down the middle. "Come on!"

Layshan stumbled behind, his mind spinning too fast to pull away.

He couldn't afford indulgences like extra blankets, pillows, and clothes. A current of anxiety ran through his mind, so overwhelming that he didn't have the mental capacity to consider what the man meant by "shower things." He'd never taken a shower before, unless he counted standing beneath the sloped corner of an awning during a summer storm to catch the runoff.

He glanced over his shoulder at the man, who gave him a small smile, eyes twinkling with mischief.

"Good luck," he called.

# CHAPTER 3

Ra stopped before the metal part of the wall and shoved his thumb into a button beside it. A moment later, the metal parted, revealing a small room on the other side. Ra jumped inside, but Layshan took his time, poking his head into the small room. He toed the line between worlds, trying to understand the purpose of such a room.

Ra waved him forward. "Hurry up. The doors will close."

Layshan jumped inside on instinct as the wall shut, unsure what exactly he was committing to. He spun, the walls too narrow and claustrophobic, and the whole thing jerked. The floor seemed to fall out from under him. Panic filled his lungs, forcing itself through his magic until he jumped, his air pushing him higher. But when his head collided with the ceiling, he crashed back down to the floor in a heap.

Ra crumpled in a fit of laughter, but Layshan froze, unsure how to react. The room quaked around them, but everything *looked* normal, and Ra was unconcerned.

"You should have seen the way you hit the ceiling!" Ra cried, tears rolling down his cheeks as he gasped for breath. "It was like, *Oh no*! And then *crash*!" He punctuated every word with waves of his hands and exaggerated noises.

Layshan scowled, but it only made Ra laugh harder. Layshan flicked his hand, sending Ra's clean white shirt flying over his obnoxious laughing face.

Ra giggled as he fixed his shirt, giving a half-hearted "Hey!"

Layshan continued to scowl, eyes narrowing.

Ra wiped at the tears on his cheeks. "Oh, come one. It was funny!"

Layshan huffed through his nose, rubbing at the sore spot on his head.

Ra grabbed his hand and helped him stand. "We're almost there. And to make it up to you, I'll give you my roll if there are any."

Layshan grunted his best *you better* when the doors opened again. Long tables filled the room on the other side instead of the beautifully decorated room from before. People of all ages gathered in groups more occupied with talking than eating. The roar of their combined voices filled the room. No one looked up at them as they entered, unbothered by new people coming and going.

Ra led Layshan to the far side of the room, where the most amazing scents wafted. Some were warm and comforting, like bakery bread and pubs serving hot stew. Others were sweet, a mix of sun-ripened berries and fruits Layshan couldn't identify, the scents of a market in the morning when barrels were still overflowing and the pastries were fresh. The magic in his chest lifted with his spirits, pulling the scents closer on a breeze of his own making.

Food lined the back of the room, and various savory dishes were laid out next to fresh vegetables and whipped potatoes—things Layshan had only ever seen and never eaten. His mouth watered, and his fingers fidgeted, eager to reach out and stuff it all into his mouth.

An older Witch and Anima stood behind the row of food, discussing what to do with the leftovers and what should be put out after dinner. Layshan waited for them to shoo the boys away or demand payment, but neither of them gave their approach much notice.

Ra grabbed two metal trays and pushed one into Layshan's hands. He started down the line, scooping spoonfuls of savory stew, whipped potatoes, and a small mound of green vegetables. He was at the end of the line when he realized Layshan's tray was still empty.

"You haven't gotten anything. Aren't you hungry?" Ra said around a mouthful of potato, already spooning food into his mouth.

Layshan took a step closer and whispered, "I can't. I don't have enough money."

Ra's head tipped, trying to determine if Layshan was joking. "You don't need money. It's part of living here. Take as much as you want."

Layshan shook his head. "I haven't earned anything yet."

"But you will. And you can't work if you starve to death. Here, you eat meat?" Layshan gave a hesitant nod. Ra spooned a heaping mound of meaty stew onto the tray, the brown gravy speckled with dark bits of pepper and other spices. The overwhelming scent tore at Layshan's resolve.

Panic seized his heart, his mouth drying when he realized the Witch and Anima were eyeing him.

"Stop it," he squeaked. "You're going to get me in trouble!"

Ra ignored him. "You need potatoes, too."

As Ra scooped a mountain of butter-scented potatoes onto Layshan's tray, the Anima woman walked over, watching him closely.

That was it. Ra was nice, but he lived in luxury for too long. He didn't understand that kids like Layshan couldn't take food without paying, and now he would be kicked out before he stole his first coin. His knuckles turned white as he gripped the metal tray, prepared to run and take the food with him.

"What's going on here, Ra? You find someone new?"

Ra nodded, licking gravy off his thumb. "Yes, ma'am. But he thinks he's going to get in trouble."

The Anima sighed, shaking her head, hands resting on her hips. "I swear, that man always finds the skinniest of them," she muttered, looking Layshan up and down. "Look at you, scared to death."

She came around and stopped before Layshan. He waited for her to take his tray, but nothing in Thaumoria could tear it from his hands now that it carried delicious-smelling food. He'd fight, scream, and run before letting her take it.

She crouched, getting at eye level. "Dear, I promise you won't get in trouble for taking food here, okay? It's already paid for, so take as much as you want. If anyone tries to tell you otherwise, you tell them Ms. Helen said it's okay, but you won't have any problems here."

Layshan looked for the lie in her red-brown eyes but found nothing but sincerity and warmth. Gaze bouncing between her and the tray of vegetables, he tried to decide if he could reach out and take it.

"Go on," she prodded.

Hesitantly, he grabbed the spoon. Muscles tensing, he prepared for the yelling and demand of payment in any form he could offer. But she didn't say a word, only smiled encouragingly. He scooped out a few pieces, put them on his tray, and met her eyes again, questioning everything.

"Good." Nodding, she reached out and pushed dirty hair out of his eyes. Layshan flinched when her fingers met his temple, preparing to be struck but trusting her not to. "You eat, then clean up and get some sleep." The words were an order, yet somehow still filled with a motherly comfort he savored. Layshan nodded his understanding. One more sweet smile and returned to her conversation with the Witch.

"Ready?" Ra plopped a browned roll peppered with various seeds into Layshan's heap of potatoes.

Layshan nodded.

Ra led him between the long tables stretching from one end of the room to the other, lined with benches on both sides occupied by scattered clumps of people. Layshan eyed every one of them as he passed. Ms. Helen's name sat on the tip of his tongue, ready to defend him if anyone accused him of not belonging, but no one paid him any mind.

Ra guided them to a mostly empty section where a girl about twelve years older than them and a younger girl about six years younger sat far away from everyone else.

Ra sat across from the girls and started arranging his tray. Layshan hesitated, but Ra patted the seat beside him and ordered, "Sit."

So Layshan did.

He studied the girls, neither of whom said a word, trying to figure out what they were.

The older girl was made of hard metal, with silver hair, colorless skin, and metallic eyes. She wore a sleeveless shirt, showing off well-toned arms. When her eyes met his, they were cold as a coin in winter, revealing no kindness.

The younger girl looked both exactly and nothing like the older one; they had the same features but in different colors. With brassy hair and matching eyes, she bounced as she dug into her potatoes, waving at Ra with a gloved hand. While the older girl showed off her muscles, fabric covered the younger from the neck down. Aside from her head, not a single bit of skin showed.

"Layshan, these are my friends. Malaina," he gestured to the fierce girl of silver, "and Lybbi," gesturing to the younger brassy one.

Layshan swallowed hard, scared to meet those cold eyes again. But the man's words played on a loop through his mind.

*You should think about investing in some friends.*

Ra had the potential to be a good friend, and if he said the girls were his friends, then maybe Layshan should put in an effort he never had before.

Friends could be good. Friends meant safety and security.

He cleared his throat, staring at his tray so hard he might glare right through to the table. His voice squeaked as he spoke up. "So… do you… steal stuff, too?"

Malaina's head whipped up, her eyes a freshly sharpened knife to his heart. He wasn't sure what magic class she was, but she couldn't be a Fire Wielder because that look said he'd be up in flames already if she were.

"No," she bit, voice as sharp as her metallic eyes.

Layshan's shoulders hunched beneath her venom, and he continued to stare at his food, not saying another word.

That was enough making friends for him.

"Malaina," Ra sighed, exasperated. "Don't scare this one off. I like him."

Malaina stuck her tongue out at Ra in a gesture too young for someone so intense. Ra, fearless, stuck his out right back.

Layshan wasn't sure what was happening. He'd never had friends before. Never had someone to jest with. Maybe cold words and mocking gestures were signs of friendship in this weird place where food was free and wealthy men offered starving kids jobs.

So, trying to fit in, he stuck out his tongue. It hung like a stray dog's drinking from a puddle. He looked at Ra to check if he was doing it right, but Ra only laughed again.

"See? He's hilarious."

Malaina scowled at them, and Layshan pulled his tongue back in, cheeks burning from embarrassment. Malaina stacked Lybbi's empty tray on hers, balanced them on one hand, and took Lybbi's fingers with the other.

"Let's go." The words came out far sweeter when directed at the small girl, almost parental.

Lybbi hopped up and waved goodbye to both Ra and Layshan. Layshan gave a small wave back, a slight bend of his fingers peeking over the table's edge, and pressed his lips into his best imitation of a smile.

Malaina glared and hauled Lybbi away toward an exit.

"You have weird friends," Layshan said quietly.

Ra shrugged and returned to his dinner, unaffected by the judgment. "Normal friends are boring."

Layshan wasn't sure he agreed with that, but given his lack of experience, he wasn't in a place to argue.

Instead, he took a big bite of his stew to keep his hands busy. The flavors melted on his tongue, distracting him with ecstasy. He wanted to cry at the salt, meat, and gravy coating his mouth, as warm and thawing as the first rays of summer sun after a harsh spring. It was the best thing he'd ever eaten, and he couldn't stop shoveling in one mouthful after another.

For the first time, he realized how little he'd eaten in his life, and a sinkhole opened inside him. It swallowed the food whole, leaving him empty and wanting more. His stomach stretched to accommodate everything but the tray, clawing at him, begging for more.

"You're going to be sick if you don't stop," Ra warned him blandly, as though he already knew the words were useless.

As quickly as the food went down, it came back up. Layshan broke out in a cold sweat, his entire body rejecting the contents he'd forced into it.

Ra pointed. "There's a bin over there."

Layshan ran, barely making it to the can before undigested chunks and stomach acid scorched his throat, finding their way into the can and up his nose. An eternity of heaving later, his stomach was empty again, leaving him shaking, hair drenched in sweat, and muscles aching. He fell to his knees, holding the bin for dear life in case he started hurling again.

Someone kneeled beside him, and when he looked over, he found Ra holding a glass of water and a roll. He glanced around to see how much of a scene his being sick made, but of the few people still left in the room, the only ones watching him offered pitying but knowing expressions. They all looked away when he met their gaze, and he sensed he wasn't the first to puke up their first meal.

"I tried to warn you," Ra sighed, holding out the glass of water. "It's kind of a rite of passage. Most people eat too much on their first night. You'll be okay."

Layshan swished the water through his teeth and spat it into the bin before gulping half in one swallow. Ra raised an eyebrow in warning, and he drank the rest in sips.

"Good. Now eat this. It'll help."

Layshan took a bite of the roll, which helped calm his roiling stomach. Ra sat cross-legged next to him despite the proximity of the smelly can, patiently waiting for him to finish.

"If you think you can handle another, I promised you mine, too. But don't get sick again, or you won't sleep well."

Layshan nodded, understanding. He finished his roll, savoring the flaky, soft inside and half of Ra's before they left the dining hall.

# CHAPTER 4

After dinner, Ra showed Layshan the kids' dorm.

"This is where kids under sixteen, who haven't started working or have just started, stay. You can move into a private apartment once you can afford the rent."

The dorm had a boys' and girls' side, each with an enormous bathroom. Ra gave Layshan soap for his body and hair, towels, and clean clothes and then pointed him toward a shower stall.

Layshan spent more time standing in the rain of hot water than cleaning himself, watching the dirt swirl around his feet. He even took the time to run a finger through the steam, his air creating simple shapes out of the fog. He didn't have enough control of his magic to do much more and wasn't sure he was capable of more.

But magic was as much a part of him as his name was, and on the rare mornings when Layshan had nothing to do and a heavy mist blew in off the ports to hang over the city, he'd practiced shaping it. Shaping fog and mist gave substance to his magic, something with a physical form he could hold in his hand.

Eventually, he stepped out of the shower and changed into soft, clean clothes, the fabric hanging off his bony frame.

An unrecognizable reflection stared back at Layshan in the bathroom mirror. The only time he'd ever seen himself was when he caught sight of a dull image reflected in the store windows of a scraggly child slinking past shoppers. The clean, unwarped version was uncanny.

Layshan wondered if his hair had always been so blonde or if the soap had done something weird to it. He'd never seen it without being coated in grease and dirt, even after dunking it in a puddle or sitting under drainpipes. He couldn't stop touching it, the downy softness foreign to him. It hung longer than he remembered, and he pushed it in different directions to see how various styles changed the angles of his unfamiliar, gaunt face.

After a while, though, he couldn't keep his eyes open. He might've fallen asleep standing up, staring into the mirror, but he wouldn't pass up his first opportunity to sleep in an actual bed.

Layshan gathered the fluffy towels, holding them close to his chest, and entered the boy's dorm. Wooden bunk beds lined the walls, but only half were occupied. Some boys opted for their own bunks, while others shared, hanging over the edges to talk to one another.

He found Ra on a bottom bunk in the back corner, lying atop a colorful quilt, playing with the two copper coins he always had.

Face splitting into a toothy grin, he sat up, giving Layshan a good once over. "Look at you. No dirt, and you're still alive. It's a miracle."

Layshan scowled, but it was half-hearted at best. He was getting used to how Ra teased without being mean. There was never any judgment in his jokes, like he only wanted to bring light to whatever situation he was in.

Looking around, Layshan wasn't sure which bunk to take. The claimed ones had blankets and pillows piled on top, whereas the empty ones had bare mattresses. Layshan set his towels on an empty bunk next to Ra's, and Ra made a face at him.

"What are you doing?"

Layshan snatched his towels and soaps back, cradling them against his chest. Someone must've claimed the bunk, though it sure didn't look like anyone was planning on sleeping there. Maybe Ra didn't want him so close. He looked around for one by itself, deciding on one against the opposite wall, and started toward it.

"Where are you going?" Ra's voice rose in pitch, sounding sad. Almost hurt.

Layshan stopped, running a thumb worriedly against the soft fibers of the towel, confused. Was a bunk assigned to him that he didn't know about? Maybe they were sending him to a different dorm for the kids who might not last. The ones so new the man was still considering their worth.

Ra climbed out of his bottom bunk, standing on the mattress to inspect the made-up bunk above. "Is something wrong with the one I made for you? Do you want the bottom? We can switch. I tried to find a really good pillow for you."

*Oh…*

The bed was made… for him. While his introductory duties were over, Ra wasn't throwing him away. He wanted Layshan nearby, and he wanted to share.

Concern bunched Ra's brows as he inspected the top bunk, looking for any reason Layshan wouldn't want it.

Tears sprung to Layshan's eyes, and his throat tightened. He couldn't remember the last time he'd cried, but it wouldn't be now, in front of all these kids he didn't know. He swallowed down the tears and walked back over.

"It looks great," he assured Ra quietly.

Ra let out an exaggerated breath, cheeks puffing out. "Oh, good. I thought I'd screwed it up."

"No. It's perfect."

"Awesome!" Ra jumped down from his mattress and went to the end of the bed, where two trunks sat.

"So, this one," he pointed to the one on the right, "is mine, and the other is yours. We can find a lock if you want one, but no one steals in the dorms. We all have what we need, and no one wants to risk getting kicked out."

Layshan dumped his newfound possessions into the trunk. His fraying little coin pouch sat in the corner where Ra must have put it. The towels and soaps so looked inconsequential sitting in the trunk, and for a moment, Layshan looked forward to the prospect of filling it with new things. Aside from his dirty clothes and little coin pouches, he'd owned nothing worth keeping. He stamped down the hope as quickly as it rose, not wanting to get too attached to a place that might not last.

He climbed the sturdy ladder onto his bed. *His* bed. It was still a weird concept. The mattress sunk under his weight, and the fuzzy blanket had a satiny edge that slipped between his fingers. The entire structure shook when he flopped onto the mattress, but he couldn't make himself care as he sunk into a cloud. He pulled the pillow closer, scrunching and bunching it against his face, moaning into the fluffy good-ness. The pillow, blanket, and mattress… all smelled so… clean. Like soap, berries, and something else floral, a scent he recognized wafting out of apothecary shops that eased both his mind and his magic.

Ra laughed. "I was going to say we should find you clothes for tomorrow, but I think I'll give you and your pillow time together. I sprayed it with some of Jade's sleep stuff to help with first-night jitters."

The mention of more clothes caught Layshan's attention. He'd never owned two full outfits before.

He peered over the railing of his bed, down to where Ra sat on his colorful quilt, and pulled at the collar of his new shirt.

"I have clothes," he muttered.

Ra shook his head. "Those are sleep clothes. You'll need clothes for training, too."

Layshan studied the shirt, baffled. If you're tired enough, all clothes are sleep clothes, and he couldn't figure out what made these special.

Peering back over the railing, Layshan became mesmerized by Ra's quilt and all its mismatched fabrics. The collage was so different from anything else in the dorm. No other bunk had a quilt, and this one looked handmade.

He pointed down. "Your blanket…"

Ra grinned from ear to ear, eyes going distant and soft, lost in a safe memory. "My mom made it for me."

Layshan's jaw hung open. "Your…"

Ra's chest puffed with pride. "Uh-huh. She gave it to me last year."

A deep longing tugged at Layshan's stomach, a need buried so deep he didn't realize it existed. A mom… Ra had a mom. He looked around at the other boys, wondering how many of them knew their moms and dads and if he was the only one who didn't. He had parents. Of course he did. He came from somewhere. Children didn't just pop out of the earth for the sole purpose of being trampled on by society. But he didn't know who they were. They definitely weren't visiting him and making him blankets.

"You know your mom?" He couldn't stop the words from slipping out, coated in something heavy. A syrupy sadness he couldn't ignore now that it had risen.

Ra beamed, not hiding the love pouring from him. "She's going to come get me one day. And then we're going to live together, and I won't ever have to steal anything ever again."

A bitter laugh broke through Ra's daydream.

"Are you still talking about that slut you call a mom?" a large boy mocked from the end of the bunk.

Instantly, Layshan's defenses went up, his walls slamming into place. Something about the boy reminded him of Dai, from the jeer in his voice to the sneer on his face. He especially disliked how he talked to Ra or about his mom. It set every nerve in his body alight and ready to fight.

Anyone with a mom who made them quilts deserved to be proud. If Layshan had a mom or a dad, he'd never stop talking about them. He'd climb the rooftops and scream it to the winds, if only for someone to hear.

Ra nodded, unaffected by the boy's malice. "Of course. She's going to come for me. You'll see."

The boy snorted. "Yeah, right. You're stupid if you think that's true."

"Maybe, but I don't think so."

"That's because you're stupid, and stupid people don't think." The boy laughed at his terrible joke, a mocking sound that grated against Layshan's skin and made his lip curl.

The boy spotted Layshan peeking over the top bunk. "You find yourself a pet?"

Layshan's temper flared in his veins, but Ra

didn't care about how awful this boy was being. "He's my new friend."

The boy rolled his eyes. "Whatever. Where's my cut?"

Ra tipped his head with a mask of innocence. "You're cut of what, Rodan?"

Rodan leaned in close, looming over Ra's small form closer than Layshan cared for. "You know what. You can either hand it over, or I'll beat it out of you in training tomorrow."

Ra shrugged and stood from the bed, pushing past the boy and heading for his trunk. Layshan watched from above as Ra opened his trunk and pulled out a bulging coin pouch. He dumped some coins into his hand and tossed them up and down, just high enough to clink and jingle without dropping a single one.

"You know what the Anima say, don't you?" Ra closed his fingers around the coins and waved his hand.

Rodan rolled his eyes, his entire head rolling with them, as if Ra were a crick in his neck he was trying to displace. "No. What?"

"You catch more badgers with honey." Ra tossed the coins back and forth. If his ashy brown hair and eyes weren't enough sign of him being a Kinetic, how the coins moved quickly through the air in complicated patterns would have solidified it.

"It's flies, stupid. You catch more *flies* with honey," Rodan growled.

Ra clasped his hands together, the coins jingling. "Oh, right. I'm so glad you're here to correct me. You deserve these." He opened his hands and dropped a noticeably smaller stack into Rodan's waiting palm.

"Just remember that." Rodan pocketed the coins and headed to the opposite end of the dorms.

When he was out of earshot, Layshan leaned over further, nearly falling out of his bunk. "Who was that? Why would you give him all your money?"

"That's my partner. Everyone gets one. It's the person you do all your jobs with and who you train with the most." Ra returned to his trunk and pulled a small pile of coins from his pocket. "But I didn't give him all my money."

He shoved the leftover coins deep into an extra pillowcase before closing the trunk again.

Layshan didn't know what question to ask next. Is this normal? Is this how all partners treat each other? Because if so, he didn't want one. He dealt with enough bullies in his life, and he would not deal with them here, too.

Ra must have seen all the questions racing across Layshan's face because he stepped closer and lowered his voice. "Most partners are best friends, but I wasn't so lucky. It's ok. He's not very smart."

"But it's your money."

Ra shrugged. "I don't need much. I just want some to give my mom when she comes. Until then, I can deal."

"But…" Layshan wanted to argue. Wanted to walk right over to Rodan and take Ra's money back. Ra had been kind and patient and had a mom he was saving for. He deserved to keep everything he earned.

Ra cut him off with a smile. It wasn't the secretly sad smile of someone pretending to be okay, but the bright, beaming smile of someone truly unbothered. "It's fine, really. It will all work out one day."

"You should fight back," Layshan hissed.

Ra shook his head. "It's not worth it. Like I said, it'll all work out. Let's go to bed."

Without waiting for Layshan to respond, Ra climbed into his bunk and nuzzled under his quilt, pulling it up to his chin. Layshan laid back, crawling under his blanket, fingers finding the satiny edge and rubbing it repeatedly.

At first, he was so angry he thought he'd never fall asleep. Hot, livid blood pulsed through him, burning him from the inside out. He couldn't believe he was in a place that seemed so good, and yet people like Ra were still being bullied out of their money.

He decided Rodan was being selfish and hated him for it.

Despite his raging temper, Layshan fell asleep, soothed by the floral scent dancing around him. The last thing he remembered thinking before falling into the black abyss of sleep was that he wouldn't sit by and watch next time.

# CHAPTER 5

Ra practically dragged Layshan down the stairs from the dining hall to what he called the "training room" the next night. Apparently, most of the guild operated on backward hours. Waking in the evening and sleeping with the sun meant twilight breakfasts and dawn bedtimes.

Layshan hadn't been eager to leave his bed, nestling further into the blankets when Ra tried to shake him awake. But the mention of breakfast propelled him off the top bunk, fueled by his rumbling belly. After breakfast, Ra shoved a new set of clothes into Layshan's hands and demanded he change fast so they weren't late. Late for what, Layshan didn't know.

"Cutting it a little close, are we not, Ra?" the man from the alley asked, rolling up the sleeves of his crisp button-down shirt until they sat in perfect folds at his elbows. He lifted a reprimanding eyebrow at the boys, but the rebuke was far from scathing.

Ra dipped his head, shifting from foot to foot. "Sorry, Malachi. Someone wouldn't get out of bed."

Layshan's mouth fell open, and he nudged Ra in the ribs with his elbow.

"Ow!"

Malachi's lips twitched with amusement, but his features settled quickly, taking on a more authoritative air. "I see. And what is Layshan doing here? You know the rules."

Ra's shoulders fell with the exaggerated sass of a kid too comfortable with the adult they talked to. "I know, I know. But I didn't know what else to do with him."

Malachi rolled his eyes and sighed. "That is

fine. Layshan, find a spot on the benches. You will not be participating tonight."

Layshan did as he was told, and Ra made his way over to Malaina, clad in all black, her silver hair tied back from her face. The other kids gave her a wide berth, refusing to come within two arm lengths of her. Ra sauntered right up, though, and stretched by her side, rattling off about one thing or another. Layshan couldn't help but notice Lybbi was missing and wondered if maybe she was too young. There were a few others who looked to be about her age, though.

Malachi clapped, the sound ringing louder than should be possible, making Layshan jump. "Let us get started."

For the next couple of hours, Malachi turned from a nonchalant, almost indifferent guardian to an authoritarian. He spoke commands that invited no questions, and while they weren't loud, they were quick and sharp. The kids ran through drills, from basic sprints to precise fighting forms Malachi corrected without pity, down to the most minor details, such as the angle of their foot or a bend in their knee. The entire group moved as one through the motions, little soldiers striking invisible targets, movements exact, Malachi their stoic general.

By the end, they all dripped with sweat, muscles shaking from sitting in wide-legged forms until they couldn't hold them any longer.

"Is this what training is always like?" Layshan asked Ra during one of their water breaks.

Ra grinned, taking joy in his shaky knees. "Nah, forms are easy. Wait until climbing or weapons. Those lessons are brutal, but the older kids have it worse."

The whole thing ended with what Malachi called sparring matches, which Layshan learned were practice fights. Watching the kids move in fluid motions around each other, sweeping at legs, blocking attacks, and using their magic in creative defenses, had him itching to join.

Until then, everything about the guild had been overwhelming and foreign. But fighting… fighting, he knew. Fighting he was good at. As he watched the matches, he marked which kids had a knack for it and which kids relied on practiced forms too much.

"Malaina and Nemalia up next. Center ring."

Malaina smirked and stood smoothly from her spot at the end of the bench.

Once again, everyone kept their distance from her except Ra and Layshan, who moved down to join her when everyone sat. It was like an invisible barrier that only a select few could breach surrounded her. With a predator's grace, she walked to the center ring, not a hint of apprehension on her face. She was entirely at ease with the idea of being punched and kicked. Without the clothing-clad Lybbi, she was even more terrifying, as if the young girl tamed her somehow.

Nemalia, however, looked like her life was flashing before her eyes.

Layshan leaned over to Ra. "What does Malaina do for work?"

Ra didn't think twice before answering, more focused on his coppers than the match.

"She's an assassin. That's her partner. Today, anyway."

Layshan was almost taken aback by how casually Ra said the job title. Yet, it fit Malaina well… too well. Despite her age, she looked like she'd kill for money.

"She has multiple partners?"

"No, she just goes through them really fast. People are afraid of her and don't want to work with her."

Layshan didn't blame them. The training hadn't worn on her; it had only sharpened the edge she carried. The glistening sweat on her forehead added to a deadly air. Her gleaming eyes narrowed, almost hungry for the fight about to happen.

"Just a reminder," Malachi called from beside the ring where the two girls readied. "Malaina, you may not use magic."

She nodded, seeming to only half listen to words she'd probably heard a hundred times. Her partner visibly relaxed at the reminder but still looked terrified as she prepared for the match.

"What's her magic class?" Layshan asked.

"Death Bringer," Ra stated, as though it were as common as an Elemental.

Layshan's heart stopped dead in his chest. The next thing he knew, he was on his feet, knowing he could do nothing. He was horrified for the poor girl facing the assassin and wanted to step in. Despite the man's reminder, he was sure Nemalia would die right there in front of them all.

*A Death Bringer.*

How was she even alive? A Death Bringer's magic was dark, and those with dark magic weren't allowed to live. Yet, there she was, about to touch someone. And no one was doing anything about it.

They were encouraging it.

The other kids perched on the edge of their benches, jeering at the Death Bringer. They'd sent a kitten to fight a wolf and were all eagerly waiting to witness the gory execution. No one took bets as they had with the other matches, though. It was as if they collectively agreed on who they thought would win.

Or maybe they were too scared to bet against the assassin.

Nemalia's brow dripped with sweat, and she bit her lip. She did not look as confident. Her eyes widened a hair as Malaina approached the ring. She, too, sensed the malice rolling off the silver girl in tangible waves.

Malaina raised her fists, a small arrogant smile playing at the corner of her lips as she took in her trembling partner.

On Malachi's mark, she feinted forward instead of attacking with a quick jerk of her shoulders and a shift of her feet.

That was all it took.

Nemalia scurried away, Malachi's reminder of Malaina's restriction forgotten.

The moment Nemalia's foot slipped beyond the boundary, Malaina's face split into the grin of a feral cat who'd backed a rat into a corner for the fun. Malachi called the match in Malaina's favor, and she turned, flipping her hair over a shoulder before heading back to her side of the ring.

Nemalia released a heavy breath and

slumped to the floor, chest rising and falling faster than was healthy.

Malachi hung his head, looking both disappointed and exasperated. He pinched the bridge of his nose. "Nemalia, you may return to the bench, and we will talk about this later."

Malaina smirked at the floor, trying and failing to hide her immodesty. Clearly, she took some sick pride in terrifying her partners.

"Do we have any volunteers to take on Malaina today?"

Only one person raised their hand, and Layshan's heart dropped when he realized it belonged to Ra.

Malachi waited for anyone else to offer, but no one did. "Fine," he sighed. "Ra, you are up next."

"What are you doing?" Layshan squeaked. Panic had his heart pounding in his ears as his only friend in the world willingly volunteered for his death.

Ra shrugged as he pushed to his feet and swung his arms. "She can't use her magic. It's fine."

"She could kill you."

"Yeah, but she won't." Ra was too confident for Layshan's liking, but he headed to the ring before Layshan could stop him.

Ra bounced the entire way and smiled when Malaina smirked. To Layshan's relief, the smile was more genuine than malicious. Amused at Ra's excitement rather than reveling in his fear.

"Let's go!" Ra barked, riling up the onlookers, and the other kids shouted with encouragement.

Malachi sighed, flicking his fingers at the ring as if he already knew the outcome but couldn't avoid it. "Go."

Malaina didn't throw herself into the fight. Instead, she circled, and Ra matched her step for step. When they attacked, their strikes were a choreographed dance of practiced feints and punches. Despite their familiarity, the match was still some of the most horrifying minutes of Layshan's young life. He held his breath, flinching every time skin met skin.

The only saving grace was that Malaina

seemed fond of Ra. Surely she wouldn't kill him.

Still…

Ra threw one punch wrong, and Malaina grabbed his wrist, stepped under his shoulder, and threw him to the ground with the ease of a farmer tossing a sack of potatoes.

Ra groaned.

Malaina smiled.

Malachi rubbed his face, letting out something between a chuckle and a sigh. "Okay. Malaina, back to the bench."

Malaina helped Ra to his feet before heading back to the empty end of the bench. Everyone turned to avoid her, brushing their knees as she passed.

"Another partner pairing, shall we? Rodan, you are next."

Layshan sat back on the bench, breathing a little easier once Malaina was back in her isolated corner.

Rodan stood, stretching and smiling like a menace.

Malaina let out something between a snort

and a growl; her lips curled in a snarl as she analyzed Rodan's every movement.

"That guy is the worst," she murmured to no one in particular, but Layshan sensed she was talking to him. He was tempted to agree but didn't want to garner a speck of her attention. He'd rather have a common enemy with the only Death Bringer in Thaumoria than attract her wrath.

Rodan entered the sparring ring, a twisted toothy smile curling his face into something hideous. Conversely, Ra was nothing but good-natured energy, bouncing on the balls of his feet.

"Go."

The match lasted longer than the one with Malaina, but it went nothing like Layshan expected. He expected Rodan to take advantage of the situation, as he had in the dorm, and give Ra the threatened beating.

Instead, he threw the match.

It wasn't brazenly obvious. He made a show of it, but wasn't putting his full weight into his throws.

Ra was fast. Thanks to his Kinetic magic, he moved weightlessly and took advantage of an occasional misplaced foot, pulling it out from under Rodan without laying a hand on the larger boy. But Ra wasn't *that* good. Rodan should have won, but he exaggerated every hit he took until he tapped out and let Ra claim his victory.

Malaina rolled her eyes, looking away from the match as though it disgusted her.

Malachi scrutinized every step and breath from over a finger brushing his lips.

Layshan saw the complete picture with stark clarity.

Rodan bullied Ra behind the scenes, where only a handful of people saw, then pitied him in public. It made him look like the good guy—like someone partnered with someone unworthy—giving Ra the chance to build his confidence, only to tear it down in private.

It made Layshan's blood boil. His temper reared up and settled between one heartbeat and the next. Merely looking at Rodan fueled the hurricane in his veins.

"That marks the end of training for today. Everyone, eat and rest up. Tonight was easy. Next time, we will return to weapons, and I am sure you all remember how that went last time."

The kids let out a resounding chorus of groans, some rubbing at phantom bruises. The group left, stretching and moaning about tired muscles. Layshan stood to join them, but the sound of his name stopped him.

"Layshan." His name was a crisp, commanding order on Malachi's tongue. "You will stay."

Layshan froze, anxiety coursing through him, wondering if he had done something wrong. All he did was sit there.

A hand on his arm caught his attention. Ra grinned as if he sensed Layshan's unease. "It's ok. Everyone starts alone."

Layshan was not convinced but nodded all the same. "Ok."

He didn't like the idea of being left alone with an older man he barely knew. But so far, Malachi had done nothing but show him kindness and provide him with comfort. The least

Layshan could do was offer a bit of trust in return.

Then, the room was empty, and the only sound was the lazily turning fans overhead circulating the air in barely detectable drafts.

Malachi didn't approach. He stood back, studying the dressed-up street rat like a Shifter studied a marble slab. Like Layshan was something to be carved and molded into something greater.

"Now, have you received any training regarding your magic?"

# CHAPTER 6

Layshan swallowed hard and shook his head.

"But you use it often, no?"

He shrugged, unsure what it had to do with fighting or thieving. Learning how to fight made sense. It didn't come naturally to everyone. But magic… people didn't train magic, did they? Not unless they were players in the Games. Wielding was instinctual. Air was another soul living side-by-side within his veins, residing at his fingertips and ready to be used at any moment, whether for something as mundane as blowing away an unpleasant stench or as important as redirecting a punch that would have knocked him out cold.

Malachi nodded. "Around here, we have a saying: tired magic is controlled magic. Quite a few have come to me with minimal knowledge of how to control or use their magic. Over time, it builds up, ready to escape at the first sign of heightened emotions. But magic is a finite resource within us. We can only use so much of it, and in a way, it sustains us. So, when we are tired, it is tired. Exhausting people with their first-time training guarantees their unused magic does not cause any damage to the user or those around them."

Layshan's head bobbed as Malachi talked. He'd heard no one talk about magic in such a clinical way. It was like Air Wielding was something outside him rather than who he was. It was a standard part of life; he never questioned or thought about it too hard. But he knew kids with magic so weak it might as well not exist at all. He'd never considered they might not have known how to use it.

"However, most come to me in… better shape. At least marginally healthier."

A scowl twisted Layshan's face, and he studied his exposed arms in the short-sleeved shirt Ra gave him. Every ridge of his knuckles was easily identifiable, and the bone in his wrist poked out further than he'd like, but he wasn't that skinny… was he?

"So, I am going to take a chance," Malachi continued. From what I've observed and heard, you use your Air Wielding often, which means it should not be too pent up. Are you ready?"

Layshan nodded, prepared to prove himself.

"Good. Close your eyes."

Layshan eyed Malachi, but when the man stood patiently still, he did as he was told.

"I want you to search for the source of your magic. It is different for everyone. For some, it resides deep within their stomach; others feel it in their heart or throat. It stems from somewhere, though, so I want you to find it. Do not tap into it yet. Just observe it."

Layshan searched within himself, not quite

sure what he was looking for. He'd never looked for the source of his magic before. But his magic kept him company on long, dark nights when he was alone and wasn't sure he ate enough to see the next sunrise. He'd call on it to remind himself it was there. An old friend always with him, no matter what, through the sleepless nights and the long winters. It played with him on summer days and cared for him during spring storms.

Layshan found his magic…everywhere. Racing through his veins, thumping in time with his heart, but most of all, swirling in his chest, happy to have his attention. It nuzzled at him, pouncing at the prospect of being set free.

A small shadow of a smile lifted his lips as he properly acknowledged his air for the first time. It was like he was part of the air around him, floating along in lazy circles with it. It didn't matter that it smelled of sweat and exhaustion; all that mattered was that it was there. He and the air became lost in each other as it came alive, lifting his newly clean hair and playing with the hem of his sleeves.

"Good." The praise was quiet, almost

proud, and Layshan felt Malachi's low words breathed into the surrounding atmosphere. "Now, I want you to picture yourself releasing it. Let it free for a moment and see what it does."

Layshan lifted his hands before him, picturing the swirling ball of magic in his chest cradled between his palms. Anticipation emanated from it, the energy swirling faster and faster. With effort, he released one big breath, and with it, his hold on his magic.

A blast of air exploded from his hands, colliding with his stomach and sending him flying through the room. He could do nothing but soar across the room until he crashed against the far wall. He fell to the ground in a heap, wheezing and gasping.

"Oh my… Jade!" Malachi's words echoed, foggy and muddled. Like they came through wads of cotton shoved in Layshan's ears. The room spun above him in dizzying swirls, and Layshan moaned, his ribs aching where his air assaulted him.

With strained effort, he rolled to his hands

and knees, trying and failing to clear his mind by shaking it. Piece by piece, the floor fell into place, and that's when he saw the woman kneeling before him.

Her features gradually came into focus, sharpening until he saw a face that wasn't quite scathing and not quite kind. Something between caring and scrutinizing at the same time. Her hooded dark eyes examined him with fervor.

Gentle hands cupped his cheeks, and a warmth spread from her fingers to his bones. Her Witch's magic seeped into his muscles, and everywhere it touched, it eased, soothing the aches and making his limbs heavy.

"How are you feeling?" she asked, getting straight to the point.

He groaned a noncommittal answer. He wasn't even sure what happened, let alone how he felt about it.

"Nothing's broken," she continued. "You'll be fine, but you need a full exam. Something that should have happened *before* you started training." She snapped the last sentence louder than the rest, making a point he was sure wasn't directed at him despite her unwavering attention on his face.

"That is my bad, Jade. I apologize. I thought we were in the clear," Malachi rambled, hovering nearby.

The Witch was on her feet in an instant, threateningly stepping into the man's space. Despite her small stature, Malachi stepped back.

She thrust a finger into his chest. "Don't feed me excuses, Malachi. You screwed up, and it could have cost the boy his health. Do better."

Malachi swallowed, lowering his chin to his chest like a scolded child beneath a mother's admonishment. But when his gaze found Layshan's, a layer of pride coated his guilty gray-green eyes.

"Of course. Never again. I swear."

Jade hmphed her suspicion of that promise but turned back to Layshan, helping him to his feet. She led him toward the back of the room, where a door stood open to an office, and Malachi placed a hand on his shoulder.

Layshan couldn't miss the mix of approval

and thrill gleaming in those Kinetic eyes. "You will do just fine here."

Malachi shrank beneath the scathing glare Jade shot his way, all but bearing protective teeth at him, before leading Layshan away.

# CHAPTER 7

Jade checked Layshan over in her office, muttering unfamiliar terms before jotting notes in a familiar file. Her magic worked differently each time she touched him. She never placed her hands anywhere other than the sides of his face, but one time, the magic focused on his throat, and the next time, it bounced between his ribs.

When she finished, she leaned back against her desk, crossing her arms. Despite hiding her hands, her forearms twitched as she talked. Layshan wasn't a worldly child, but even he could see the signs of a City of Witches transport.

"Well, thankfully, you seem as healthy as someone in your condition can be. There are no diseases or significant illnesses, no poorly healed bones, and no internal injuries. I want you to put on weight and properly nourish yourself before you attempt anything like that again, understand?"

Layshan nodded.

"Good. Because without proper nourishment, you can become seriously injured. And while I can heal almost anything, I have other responsibilities besides you."

Layshan nodded his understanding.

"Excellent. Do you have any questions for me?"

His first instinct was to shake his head, but Jade was so straightforward it may be his only chance to have every question answered.

He cleared his throat, voice croaky. "Who are you?"

"My name is Jade. I am the head Witch here, which means I am responsible for the health of every person here. A few other Witches report directly to me, but I handle most issues." The words were monotonous, like she read them off a business card.

Layshan nodded, trying to understand the concept of someone caring about the health of criminals. She spoke with such authoritative bluntness that he almost believed it was normal.

"I thought... I thought Malachi was in charge."

She scoffed, tipping her head to the side with insolence. Her fingers flicked with annoyance, subtly emphasizing every word. "That's debatable. On paper, yes, he is in charge, but we built this business together. Organization and training are important, but nothing is more crucial than health. You'll find that even he reports to me."

Layshan watched his feet swaying while he sat on a table, the corner of his lip lifting into the beginning of an inward smile.

He liked Jade. He got the sense she wouldn't hesitate to tell someone they were being an idiot and then turn around and tend to their wounds because it was the right thing to do.

After a moment of silence, she asked, "Any other questions?"

He shook his head.

"Okay. If you have questions, you can find me here or in Malachi's office. I have my rooms, but I am rarely there. If you stay long enough, get a little older, and start eating regularly, puberty will hit in a couple of years. Then you'll have questions. You may come to me about anything, and I will always answer to the best of my abilities. If you're old enough to ask, you're old enough to get an honest answer."

Layshan's brows knitted together, but he was already overwhelmed and didn't know where to begin. He wasn't sure what questions puberty might arouse. He wasn't even confident he knew what puberty was. But if it came from eating, he figured it couldn't be too bad.

OVER THE NEXT WEEK, Layshan got a sense of what the rest of his life would be if he stayed. Every night, he filled his belly with warm food (though he learned to slow down and stop when he was full so he wouldn't puke). His limbs ached in a surprisingly pleasant way from the basic physical training Malachi put him through, though Jade hadn't approved him for anything more strenuous than jogging and forms. Somehow, though, those simple activities exhausted him.

The best part was he always knew where he was going to sleep.

So far, nothing had made him think things weren't as good as they appeared. The hardest part had been adjusting to the guild's nocturnal schedule, but he was so tired even that wasn't so difficult.

Layshan exited the boy's dorm bathroom after his second shower of the night (he couldn't get enough of how his hair felt when clean) and found Ra lounging atop his quilt-covered bunk. Layshan's heart lifted, adding an extra pep to his steps.

Ra had been gone on a job with Rodan for the day, and Layshan was happy to have his friend back.

*Friend.*

His heart struggled to accept it, but Ra became Layshan's friend. Ra read stories from one of the guild's books each night until Layshan fell asleep, keeping away the "newbie nightmares," he said. The two thieves ate all their meals together, along with the still terrifying Death Bringer and happy little Lybbi, who he learned was Malaina's sister.

Malaina hadn't warmed to him much, but developed a begrudging tolerance for his presence. So even when Ra left, she didn't kill him for sitting at their table during breakfast.

But Ra was back, which meant Layshan got to hear all about what a job was like.

Ra sat up as Layshan approached, smiling his usual ear-to-ear grin.

"Hey! You're still alive. I worried Malaina would eat you while I was gone."

A week ago, such a comment would've

made Layshan's heart race with terror, but he was getting used to Ra's sense of humor.

Layshan hung his wet towel on the corner of the bunk and dumped everything else into his trunk before slipping into Ra's bunk. They sat cross-legged on the quilt, Ra talking and Layshan listening.

It wasn't long before a familiar grating voice interrupted them. "Hey, runt. Time to pay up."

Ra sighed, rolling his eyes. But he didn't have the energy to play games. He swung his legs over the edge of the mattress to stand.

Layshan's air fluttered to life, hammering away in his chest as his blood whirled, filling his mind with the sound of his rage.

Ra didn't deserve it. He'd suspected as much the first time Rodan stole Ra's earnings, but now he knew for sure. Ra was a good person—a true friend who always smiled and honestly believed his mom would come back for him one day, and Layshan couldn't stand to watch him sit back and tolerate such treatment.

In his week at the guild, he'd learned what a

partner was supposed to be. Most partners hardly left each other's sides. They talked, laughed, and stood up for each other. If anything, Rodan did the exact opposite of that, and if anyone in this city deserved a true partner, it was Ra.

Before he knew it, he was on his feet, standing between Ra and Rodan. "No." Layshan meant for the word to sound forceful, but instead, it came out rough and squeaky.

Rodan laughed, boisterous. Layshan's entire body heated from the embarrassment washing over him, but he didn't back down. He stared hard into the larger boy's face, willing his eyes to burn holes through his skull.

Rodan put a hand on the center of Layshan's chest and pushed him back onto the bunk. "Sit down and be quiet. Ra, control your pet."

Ra sighed through his nose. "Layshan, it's fine. Really."

Ra pushed his way to his trunk, but it wasn't fine. None of it was fine. The place was supposed to be different. People earned their place fair and square, and Rodan took advantage of all the opportunities given to him.

Layshan jumped up and shoved both hands into the bigger boy's chest, his air responding to his temper and adding more force to the blow. Rodan flew back into one of the other bunks, shaking it so hard it creaked and groaned.

Fury blazed across Rodan's face, and with a whip of his hands, Layshan and Ra's entire bunk fell, nearly crushing Layshan beneath it.

Layshan ducked between the beds, grabbing the opposite side as it fell, and thrust himself through the opening. On the other side, Layshan didn't hesitate to launch himself at Rodan. He flew faster than humanly possible, aided by an angry gust of wind.

The two boys collided, falling to the floor and rolling until Rodan ended up on top. He straddled Layshan's torso, his weight making it hard to breathe.

A fist flew at Layshan's face.

At the last second, Layshan redirected the knuckles with a quick burst of air, an old but reliable trick that almost didn't work. Rodan's fist grazed Layshan's ear.

Before he could retaliate, another fist flew, and Layshan couldn't avoid it. It was going to hit him square in the nose. He braced for the pain, but before it connected, something hit Rodan in the side, and he rolled off.

Ra tackled the bigger boy. He didn't fight; instead, he backed off, crawling away, but Rodan grabbed him by the hair, smashing his face into the floor.

Layshan saw nothing but red. Pouncing, his arm wound its way around Rodan's neck, cutting off his airway. He squeezed hard, refusing to let go as Rodan thrashed.

After a moment, Rodan's movements slowed, the nails digging into Layshan's arm, losing their ferocity as the boy lost consciousness.

"Layshan, stop!"

It took Layshan a moment to recognize Ra's voice. When he looked up, Ra's fear-filled eyes brimmed with tears. Without a second thought,

Layshan let go, and Rodan crumpled to the floor before him.

Ra dragged Layshan away from the scene by the arm.

"What are you thinking? You're going to get kicked out!" Ra cried.

Layshan knew he might. He knew little about the guild, but camaraderie was important. Malachi would never approve of fighting in the dorms, which was why kids surrounded them, watching but refusing to step in. No one wanted to risk their place in the guild by getting in the middle of things.

"You could have killed me!" Rodan roared, rubbing his throat, "Ra, control your little Air Sucking pet, or you'll be the one paying for it."

Layshan didn't think. The insult triggered something in him, drudging up years of bullying that wore on him day after day. All those years of bowing to Dai, paying for things he never asked for, and taking hate from passersby on the street when he only wanted enough coins to feed himself. It all came back to him, fueling a raging storm within.

He should've walked away, pushed it all down, and ignored the hurricane goading him. But when he looked into Ra's ashy brown eyes, he couldn't.

Turning, he punched. Knuckles met bone cartilage crunching in a way that made his skin shiver with satisfaction.

Rodan shrieked, clawing at his face as blood spurted from between his fingers.

"Stay away from him!" Layshan shouted, not recognizing his voice. He couldn't remember the last time he'd screamed—never, probably—but he couldn't hold it in. How dare Rodan exploit someone as kind-hearted as Ra?

Ra, who truly believed his mother would come for him one day. Who sat up at night and told Layshan stories until he fell asleep. Who made friends with the Death Bringer because no one else would. And who made up Layshan's bed his first night and gave him a roll when he puked up his dinner.

A couple of kids came to Rodan's side, picked him up by the arms, and led him out of the dorm.

"You will never steal from or hurt him again!" Layshan continued to scream, his words following Rodan out the door. He didn't care if Rodan came for him. Layshan could handle himself. He'd taken beatings for years and knew how to keep his head down.

Hands tugged at his arm, and there stood Ra, eyes still wet with tears. Layshan realized that the fear on Ra's face wasn't the fear of Rodan. It was the fear of Layshan.

Instantly, his temper cooled, and all the fight left him. He didn't want to scare Ra; he was protecting him.

"Why would you do that? He's going to tell on you, and you'll have to leave." Ra pleaded, voice streaky with tears.

"You deserve a better partner," Layshan whispered.

Ra shook his head, his next words dripping with disappointment. "You ruined everything."

Ra slunk back to his bunk, using a bit of magic and all his weight, attempting to get it upright.

Layshan's shoulders slumped with defeat. It

didn't matter that he had won the fight; he'd sacrificed everything to do it.

Layshan waited for guilt or remorse but couldn't bring himself to care. He'd only been at the guild a week, and he'd be just fine if they sent him back to the street. So long as Rodan never hurt Ra again.

Ra was still struggling when Layshan sulked back to the bunk. Together, they got it upright, and Ra slid under his quilt without giving Layshan another glance.

It wasn't until Layshan curled up in his bunk that he heard the faintest, "Thank you," mumbled from below.

Layshan didn't reply. He curled up tighter and let out a long breath, the emotion gripping his throat loosening.

Ra didn't hate him, and that was all that mattered.

A tear slid down Layshan's cheek, soaking into his pillow, and he reminded himself repeatedly that the whole thing was worth it before finally falling asleep.

# CHAPTER 8

As the guild awoke that night, Layshan and Ra found themselves back in Malachi's office. It seemed poetic that his time in the guild would end where it began, surrounded by the towering bookshelves. It was time for everything to come tumbling down.

Layshan and Ra slumped in the two leather chairs before Malachi's desk. The guild master's fingers drummed against the wood as he studied the two boys from the other side.

"Would either of you care to explain what

happened?" Malachi's eyes flitted from one boy to the other, waiting for either to speak.

Layshan kept his lips tightly sealed, staring at the floor.

Shockingly, Ra did too. He fidgeted, fingers twiddling with his copper coins, but no words escaped his lips.

Malachi nodded once, slow and knowing.

"I see. So, Rodan broke his nose all on his own and requested a new job for no reason at all?"

Layshan's head whipped up, studying Malachi's face for any sign of a trap.

"That is correct." Malachi sighed, adjusting in his chair. "This morning, he told me he fell out of his bunk, broke his nose, and was no longer interested in thieving. That if he could not have a new partner or a new job, he would leave." Layshan and Ra exchanged a look Malachi couldn't have missed. "I sense there is more to the story than I know. Now, would either of you care to enlighten me?"

Layshan bit his lip hard. Ra shook his head.

"Then I should assume Ra got that bruise

on his face from… also falling out of his bunk?" Malachi raised an eyebrow at the boys.

Ra sat up a little straighter, sitting on his hands and clearing his throat. "I did… fall. I had a nightmare and rolled out of my bunk."

"That is quite the coincidence."

Ra nodded again, guilt written across his face so clearly it might as well be stamped there.

Malachi sighed again, sitting forward in his chair, resting his elbows on the desk. "I am going to be honest, boys. I know a fight happened. And since it was severe enough for one of my guilders to leave, something must be done."

Layshan's heart hammered in his chest. That was it. Malachi would throw him out, and possibly Ra, too. But it would be okay because he knew how to work the streets, and he could take care of Ra. He wouldn't let a single person lay a finger on him.

"I am going to have to re-partner, Ra."

For a moment, Layshan wasn't sure he heard right. But when Malachi didn't take it back, he released a relieved breath, realizing Ra could stay. Only Layshan would leave, which was the best he could hope for.

"Layshan, how would you feel about taking over Rodan's position?"

Layshan must have lost his mind because he couldn't have heard those words correctly.

But Ra bounced up and down, his usual optimism returning.

"Really?" Ra asked.

Malachi nodded.

"I…" Layshan was going to say he didn't understand, but Ra interrupted.

"Yes. He says yes!" Ra turned, grinning once again. "Right?"

"Y-yeah. Right." Layshan agreed hesitantly.

"Excellent." Malachi leaned back in his chair again, relaxing. "Ra, you may head down to breakfast. I will send Layshan down in a moment. There are things we need to discuss."

Ra jumped to his feet. "Okay!" He turned to Layshan, still cowering in his chair. "I'll see you soon."

Malachi waved a hand, and the double

doors to the office opened enough for Ra to scurry through before closing again.

The two sat in silence for long enough for Layshan to squirm.

"Am I in trouble?" he whispered.

Malachi didn't speak for a long time, stretching out the silence.

"Not this time; however," The word was pointed, a dagger meant to draw attention. "Let me make myself extremely clear. There will be no more fighting outside the sparring ring. Is that understood?"

Layshan nodded enthusiastically.

"Good. I do not allow member-on-member violence in this guild, and I will not hesitate to remove you should it happen again."

Layshan shrank with each word, the words weighing on his shoulders until he slouched.

"I had heard rumors for a while now that Rodan was bullying Ra. However, Ra would not admit to anything, and I had nothing substantial to prove it. I intended to re-partner them anyway and was waiting for an appropriate candidate. I think you two will work well together, should you decide to stay. Do you agree?"

Layshan nodded.

"Excellent. You will fit in well here if you can keep out of trouble. Ra is a good kid but a little too softhearted sometimes. He needs someone on his side, and I expect you would happily do that."

For the first time, Layshan smiled. Honestly and wholeheartedly smiled.

"I will take that as a 'yes.' " Malachi smiled, too. It was almost fatherly in its warmth.

Layshan nodded, unable to stop the smile from growing on his face until it stretched further than it ever had before. "Yes, sir."

"Good. Now, head down to breakfast. You will start reading and writing lessons tonight. We need to get you prepared to work."

Layshan jumped up and headed for the opening doors before him. He stopped at the threshold, looking back at the man in the gray suit who had changed his life and was giving him a second chance.

"Thank you," Layshan said. He didn't know

if the words were loud enough for Malachi to hear, but his voice didn't shake or squeak as he said them.

Malachi gave him an assenting nod. "Go on."

Layshan didn't wait another second. He hurried into the grand room and down the stairs to the dining hall. When he burst through the door, he spotted Ra sitting at their usual table with Malaina and Lybbi.

Their usual table. The concept made him smile until it stretched his cheeks. He gathered his breakfast, flashing a toothy grin at Ms. Helen. Tray full, he plopped down next to Ra. Lybbi waved hello at him with gloved hands, happily chewing away on a biscuit, crumbs covering the front of her long-sleeved shirt.

Malaina studied him, looking him up and down as he dug into his eggs. "You beat the snot out of Rodan?"

Layshan shrugged, briefly meeting those silver eyes.

Her lips twisted to the side in thought.

"Good," she finally said, as close to approval as he could imagine her getting.

Layshan grinned down at his tray, long blonde hair falling over his eyes.

"You're scruffy," Lybbi's small voice piped up, breaking the tension over the table. She said it like she didn't realize or care she was criticizing criminals twice her size. "You need a haircut," she said.

Malaina snorted. Ra laughed.

Layshan beamed and felt like he belonged for the first time in his life.

# Acknowledgments

When I decided to start writing the novellas for this series, Creation of a Fated Thief was the very first one I wrote. From the moment I started writing, the words poured out, and within 3 days, the story was written. It wasn't until I started writing this novella that I realized just how dearly I loved Ra and Layshan. Creation of a Fated Thief marks the beginning of a found family that I have been living with for years, and I am grateful that you all are finally able to experience it with me.

As always, I must start my acknowledgments with my alpha reader, my biggest fan, and the man who will sell my books to a tree if it would listen: my husband. He has been so supportive, and this series wouldn't be what it is without him cheering me on. Through every midnight writing session and emotional breakdown, he has been by my side, and for that, I am forever grateful.

Next, to my editor. I came to Sydney with a tighter deadline than normal for this novella, and she didn't hesitate to help. I may write the stories, but she is truly the secret weapon in my back pocket that helps perfect them.

To my cover designers, who have brought the world of Thaumoria to life and created a cover I can't stop staring at.

To my family for being endlessly supportive. They inspire the healthy relationships in my stories, and none of these stories would be possible without their influence in my life.

Finally, to you, the reader. Being an author is a crazy rollercoaster of experiences. I spent years trying to get this series traditionally published before finally deciding to go indie, and seeing the way these stories have touched your lives has assured me I made the right decision. Readers are the life force of the publishing world, and without you, I wouldn't be able to live my dream.

Forever grateful,
A.M. Eno

# About the Author

Originally from Howell, Michigan, A.M. Eno travels full-time with her husband and two cats. In 2017, she earned her Bachelor of Science from Black Hills State University, majoring in Psychology and a minor in Sociology. As a life-long avid reader, she hopes to create worlds and characters that invite readers to fall in love and feel at home. She strives to write high fantasy series that are a safe space for people of all backgrounds.